Ms. McCaw Learns to Draw

By
Kaethe Zemach

ARTHUR A. LEVINE BOOKS
An Imprint of Scholastic Inc.

Library of Congress Cataloging-in-Publication Data

Zemach, Kaethe.
    Ms. McCaw learns to draw / by Kaethe Zemach. — 1st ed.
        p. cm.
Summary: Dudley Ellington struggles to learn anything at school, but when his very patient teacher, Ms. McCaw, is unable to draw a face on the board, he helps her figure out how to do it.
    ISBN-13: 978-0-439-82914-4
    ISBN-10: 0-439-82914-3
    [1. Drawing—Fiction. 2. Teachers—Fiction. 3. Schools—Fiction. 4. Learning disabilities—Fiction.] I. Title.
    PZ7.Z416Mrs 2006 · [E]—dc22
                        2006016465

10 9 8 7 6 5 4 3 2 1   08 09 10 11 12

The art for this book was created using pen and brush with ink and watercolor.

Book design by Becky Terhune
First edition, January 2008 · Printed in Singapore 46

Dudley Ellington had trouble in school. He wasn't very good at paying attention, and it took him a long time to learn new things. When Dudley didn't know how to do his work, he'd think about racing cars and rocket ships, and fidget in his seat.

Most teachers lost their patience with Dudley Ellington, but not Ms. McCaw, the teacher in room 10. She was the best teacher Dudley had ever had.

When Dudley didn't understand something,

Ms. McCaw would explain it over and over,

until it made sense.

And if anyone made fun of Dudley,
Ms. McCaw would ask them to stop.

Ms. McCaw taught her class about the moon and stars, volcanoes, dinosaurs, owls, and butterflies. She was so smart, the children in room 10 thought their teacher knew *everything* . . .

. . . until one day, they watched her trying to draw a person's face on the board.

She tried and tried,

and tried some more,

but finally she gave up, saying, "I just can't do it! I don't know how!"

Poor Ms. McCaw.
"No matter how hard I try," she said sadly,
"I cannot figure out how to draw a face from the side."
The children in room 10 were stunned. They sat there,
looking at their teacher.
No one knew what to do . . .

. . . until somebody called out, "Don't worry, Ms. McCaw! I'll show you how!"

As the rest of the class watched in surprise,
Dudley Ellington and Ms. McCaw changed places.

Dudley stood at the board with his heart beating fast. He had never drawn a person's face from the side before, but he knew how Ms. McCaw felt, and he wanted to help her. So, he took a deep breath and said:

"When you look at someone's face from the front, you see both eyes and both ears. But when you look at someone's face from the side, you see only one eye and one ear. From the side, you see a profile: the shape of the forehead, nose, lips, and chin."

Then Dudley picked up a pen,
and slowly drew a forehead,

and a nose.

He drew two small bumps
for the person's lips,
and a bigger bump
for the chin.

Then he drew an eye
and an eyebrow
and some curly
hair on top.

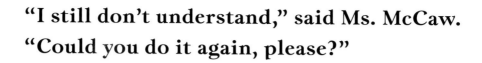

So Dudley drew another face. This one had a flat forehead and a round nose. It had a flat top lip, a bottom lip that stuck out, a long chin, and prickly hair.

But again, Ms. McCaw asked,
"Could you repeat that, please?"
So, Dudley Ellington went on drawing.

He drew someone with a big
forehead and a little nose,

and someone else with a little
forehead and a big nose.

He drew someone whose
eyes were shut,

and someone else whose
mouth was open.

Dudley drew an old person
with a wrinkly line,

a happy person
with a bouncy line,

an angry person
with a fierce line,

and an unhappy person
with a sad line.

Dudley Ellington kept on drawing, adding hair and hats and glasses and freckles . . .

. . . until the entire
board was covered.

Then Dudley gave his teacher a piece of paper and a pencil and said, "Go on, draw a forehead. Any sort of forehead. You can do it, Ms. McCaw."

When Ms. McCaw hesitated, a few kids giggled, but Dudley Ellington asked them to stop. And very slowly, Ms. McCaw drew a face from the side.

Now the teacher in room 10 was smarter than ever!
She canceled the math test that she'd been planning for
the afternoon, handed out paper and pens, and announced
that the rest of the day would be "Dedicated to Drawing!"

Thanks to Dudley Ellington!